THE SAGGY BAGGY
ELEPHANT

BY K. AND B. JACKSON
ILLUSTRATED BY
GUSTAF TENGGREN

🦌 A GOLDEN BOOK • NEW YORK
Golden Books Publishing Company, Inc., New York, New York 10106

A happy little elephant was dancing through the jungle. He thought he was dancing beautifully, one-two-three-kick. But whenever he went one-two-three, his big feet pounded so that they shook the whole jungle. And whenever he went kick, he kicked over a tree or a bush.

The little elephant danced along leaving wreckage behind him, until one day, he met a parrot.

"Why are you shaking the jungle all to pieces?" cried the parrot, who had never before seen an elephant. "What kind of animal are you, anyway?"

The little elephant said, "I don't know what kind of animal I am. I live all alone in the jungle. I dance and I kick—and I call myself Sooki. It's a good-sounding name, and it fits me, don't you think?"

"Maybe," answered the parrot, "but if it does it's the only thing that *does* fit you. Your ears are too big for you, and your nose is way too big for you. And your skin is *much*, MUCH too big for you. It's baggy and saggy. You should call yourself Saggy-Baggy!"

Sooki sighed. His pants *did* look pretty wrinkled.

"I'd be glad to improve myself," he said, "but I don't know how to go about it. What shall I do?"

"I can't tell you. I never saw anything like you in all my life!" replied the parrot.

The little elephant tried to smooth out his skin.
He rubbed it with his trunk. That did no good.

He pulled up his pants legs—but they fell right back into dozens of wrinkles.

It was very disappointing, and the parrot's saucy laugh didn't help a bit.

Just then a tiger came walking along. He was a beautiful, sleek tiger. His skin fit him like a glove.

Sooki rushed up to him and said:

"Tiger, please tell me why your skin fits so well! The parrot says mine is all baggy and saggy,

and I do want to make it fit me like yours fits you!"

The tiger didn't care a fig about Sooki's troubles, but he did feel flattered and important, and he did feel just a little mite hungry.

"My skin always did fit," said the tiger. "Maybe it's because I take a lot of exercise. But . . ." added the tiger, ". . . if you don't care for exercise, I shall be delighted to nibble a few of those extra pounds of skin off for you!"

"Oh no, thank you! No, thank you!" cried Sooki. "I love exercise! Just watch me!"

Sooki ran until he was well beyond reach.

Then he did somersaults and rolled on his back. He walked on his hind legs and he walked on his front legs.

When Sooki wandered down to the river to get a big drink of water, he met the parrot. The parrot laughed harder than ever.

"I tried exercising," sighed the little elephant. "Now I don't know what to do."

"Soak in the water the way the crocodile does," laughed the parrot. "Maybe your skin will shrink."

So Sooki tramped straight into the water.

But before he had soaked nearly long enough to shrink his skin, a great big crocodile came swimming up, snapping his fierce jaws and looking greedily at Sooki's tender ears.

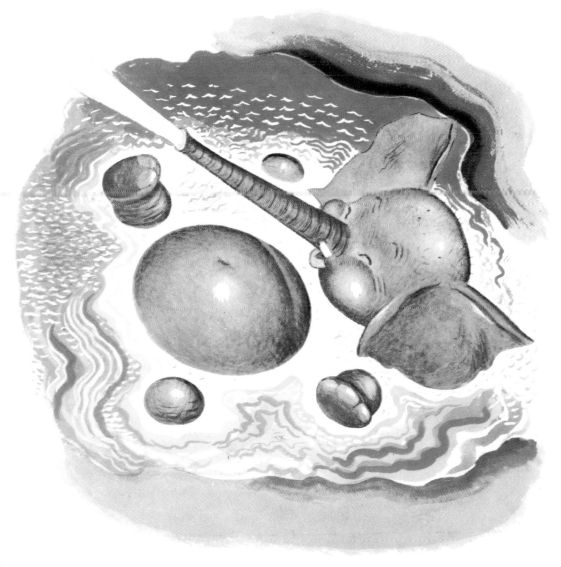

The little elephant clambered up the bank and ran away, feeling very discouraged.

"I'd better hide in a dark place where my bags and sags and creases and wrinkles won't show," he said.

By and by he found a deep dark cave, and with a heavy sigh he tramped inside and sat down.

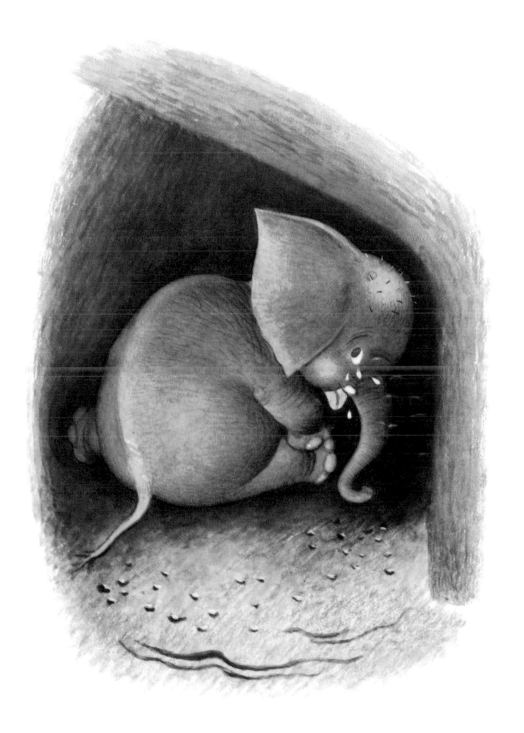

Suddenly, he heard a fierce growling and grumbling and snarling. He peeped out of the cave and saw a lion padding down the path.

"I'm hungry!" roared the lion. "I haven't had a thing to eat today. Not a thing except a thin, bony antelope, and a puny monkey—and a buffalo, but such a tough one! And two turtles, but you can't count turtles. There's nothing much to eat between those saucers they wear for clothes! I'm *hungry!* I could eat an *elephant!*"

And he began to pad straight toward the dark cave where the little elephant was hidden.

"This is the end of me, sags, bags, wrinkles and all," thought Sooki, and he let out one last, trumpeting bellow!

Just as he did, the jungle was filled with a terrible crashing and an awful stomping. A whole herd of great gray wrinkled elephants came charging up, and the big hungry lion jumped up in the air, turned around, and ran away as fast as he could go.

Sooki peeped out of the cave and all the big elephants smiled at him. Sooki thought they were the most beautiful creatures he had ever seen.

"I wish I looked just like you," he said.

"You do," grinned the big elephants. "You're a perfectly dandy little elephant!"

And that made Sooki so happy that he began to

dance one-two-three-kick through the jungle, with all those big, brave, friendly elephants behind him. The saucy parrot watched them dance. But this time he didn't laugh, not even to himself.